Derbin:
Races His Bike

Joseph Schliesman

This book is dedicated to my three little nuts-
Alekzander, Arabella and Adelyn.
May God always bless you.

I would also like to thank my wife for loving support and encouragement.

The illustrations in this book are a combination of pen and ink
colored with watercolor on cold press watercolor paper. Photoshop was used
to clean and prepare the artwork after photographing.
The text type is 14-point Avenir Book.

For written consetnt, questions or comments please email the author at:
jrs2art@gmail.com
http://jrs2art.blogspot.com

ISBN
ISBN-13: 978-1-5085-3404-4

Well, Well.

Will you look at Derbin! He just bought a new bicycle. Other cyclists have told him about the many cycling events in his area. On his last trip out, Derbin learned that people race their bikes and Derbin wants to do that too!

Right now, Derbin is on his way to the bike shop;
let's join him on his adventure.

"Hi Dan, I was out riding and some friendly cyclists told me about racing. I would like to try, where should I start?" Derbin asked. Dan was the local Bike Shop owner and race team captain.

"Well for starters, you have a cyclocross bike. It's kind of like a road bike with knobby tires," Dan Replied.

He then added, "Let's take a look at the bike and its parts. This is important if you ever need to talk to someone about your bike."

Lots of fun parts!

What's your favorite?

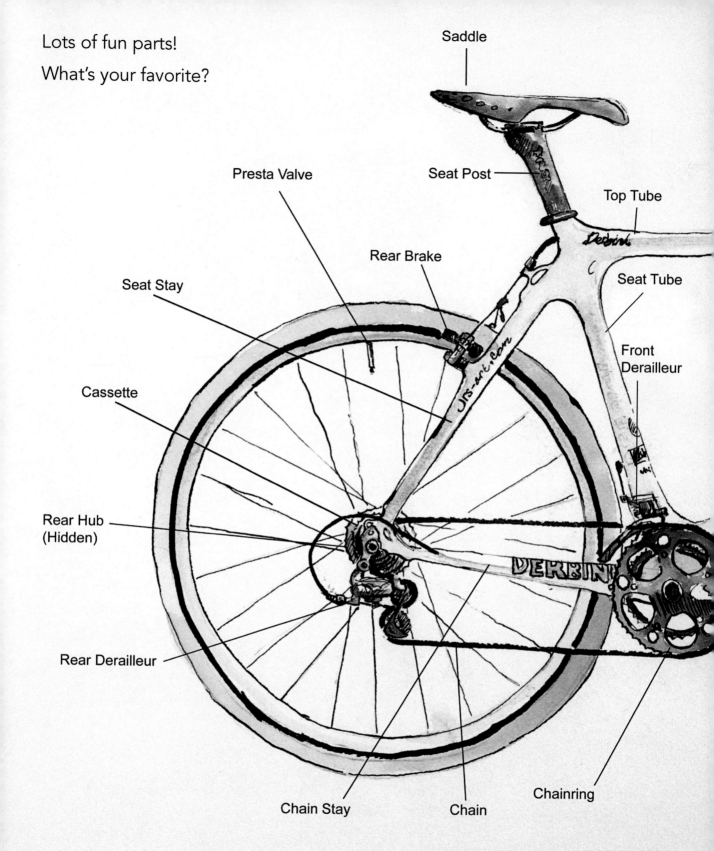

Saddle

Presta Valve

Seat Post

Top Tube

Rear Brake

Seat Tube

Seat Stay

Front
Derailleur

Cassette

Rear Hub
(Hidden)

Rear Derailleur

Chainring

Chain Stay

Chain

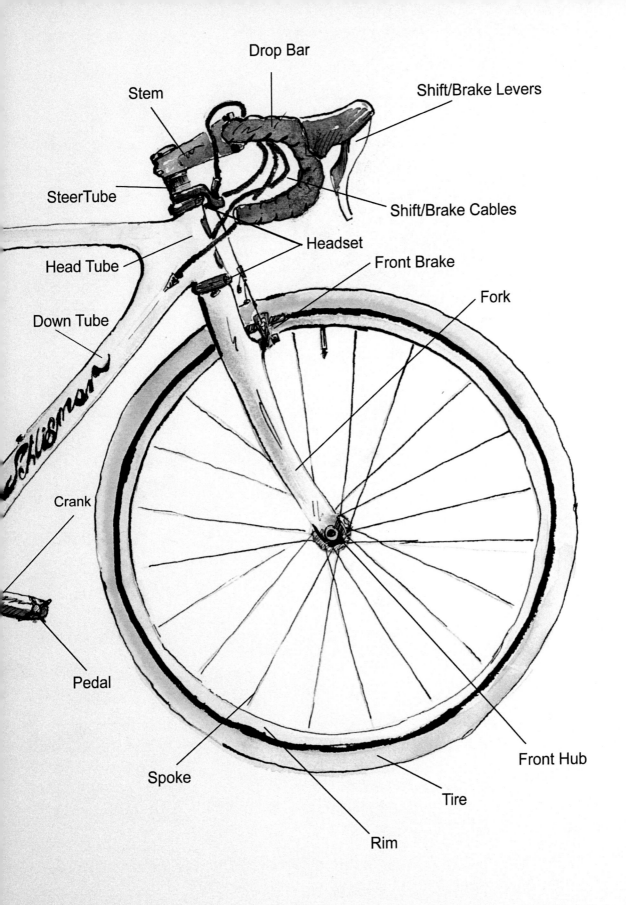

Drop Bar

Stem

Shift/Brake Levers

SteerTube

Shift/Brake Cables

Head Tube

Headset

Front Brake

Down Tube

Fork

Crank

Front Hub

Pedal

Spoke

Tire

Rim

Dan said, "Derbin you should enter a youth cyclocross race." He then explained, "Here in our area we have perfect weather for Cyclocross. People say they have more fun when it's muddy!"

"Let's look at the calendar Derbin. In two weeks there is a big race in the park. We practice in that same park. Can you practice with us?" Dan asked.

"I will ask my Mom," Said Derbin excitedly. Then as fast as he could, he ran out the door and rode home.

Ok, Ready!

That next day Derbin practiced at the park. There was a lot to learn. Things like jumping off the bike, then picking it up and running over boards called barriers. Even running up a hill with the bike. It was hard and Derbin was scared, he didn't want to look bad.

He decided practicing was not fun. He told himself that he could run up the hill anytime, and fast if he wanted. So, he left when no one was looking.

When Derbin got home he felt upset.

He told his Dad that he was scared he would
look bad and couldn't win.

Derbin's Dad thought for a moment, then said, "Learn to think of the positive things Derbin, and I think you will see that the biggest challenge in the race isn't winning." Then he added, "There is more to it then winning, you'll see. All you need is a little faith."

Derbin's mother would be home soon, so they went inside to make dinner. Derbin was still concerned, but he felt a little better. Making dinner with his Dad always cheered him up.

It was a cold, foggy and rainy Saturday morning, typical for early November.   Derbin and his Dad arrived at the course early.
To Derbin's surprise, there was a great gathering of cyclists, young, old, boys and girls; all on bikes.

At the park, a maze like course was laid out. Like a long, curving snake it wound through the grass, under trees and over hills. Derbin had no idea what to do, but he could see the bike shop tent off in the distance.

Derbin was feeling quite awkward and shy, with a fluttering
in his stomach. Derbin finally made it to the tent and found Dan. Dan
introduced Derbin to all the other kids and adults.

Dan asked Derbin if he wanted to warm up for his race, which started in a short time.

On the course Derbin exclaimed, "This is thick MUD!"

Dan puffed, "Ya, it is …. but there is a section of road and some grass…"

Derbin started to worry about the race and was wishing he had practiced more.

Along the winding and twisting course they came to the run-up section. Dan said, " Now, jump off your bike while your moving, then run up the hill with your bike on your back… just like practice!"

Dan made it look so easy.

Derbin felt silly, but he managed to make it up.

A short while later, Dan raced the Masters Category race.
"GO! Dan!" Derbin shouted as he rang his cowbell.

After Dan's race, Derbin went back to get dressed and warm up his legs. Derbin was so excited, nervous and a little scared. His race was next!

Before long, junior racers were
being called up to the start line.

The junior racers were rumbling with excitement.

"Just ride, just win," Derbin kept saying.

"Racers ready! 3,2,1" – **BANG!** Went the start gun and they scrambled off.

It was a fast and furious pace. Derbin was frantically pedaling to keep up. Mud was flying in all directions. Just then, the sky turned a dull grey and poured rain. Derbin's spirits sank. He pedaled harder. So hard that he made it up to the front, but his legs burned and his lungs felt hot. After what seemed like forever, he completed his first lap.

On the second lap the rain was heavy. The mud, thick and creamy like pancake batter. A large puddle formed and racers were falling into it. "This is GREAT!" screamed a girl as she plunged quickly in and then out of the deep chocolate colored pool. Derbin's heart sank lower, he spent all his energy trying to get up front. Now he was feeling drained and he ached all over.

Whoosh! Derbin crashed in the puddle. "I am not going to win!" Derbin cried. To make matters worse, his tire was flat. "What now?" Derbin sobbed, feeling alone.

Derbin wiped the mud from his face and noticed that a bunch of bikes were lining the race course with people running all about. To his surprise, his Dad was there, waving his arms and saying, "Get in the pit and get a new wheel! Hurry!"

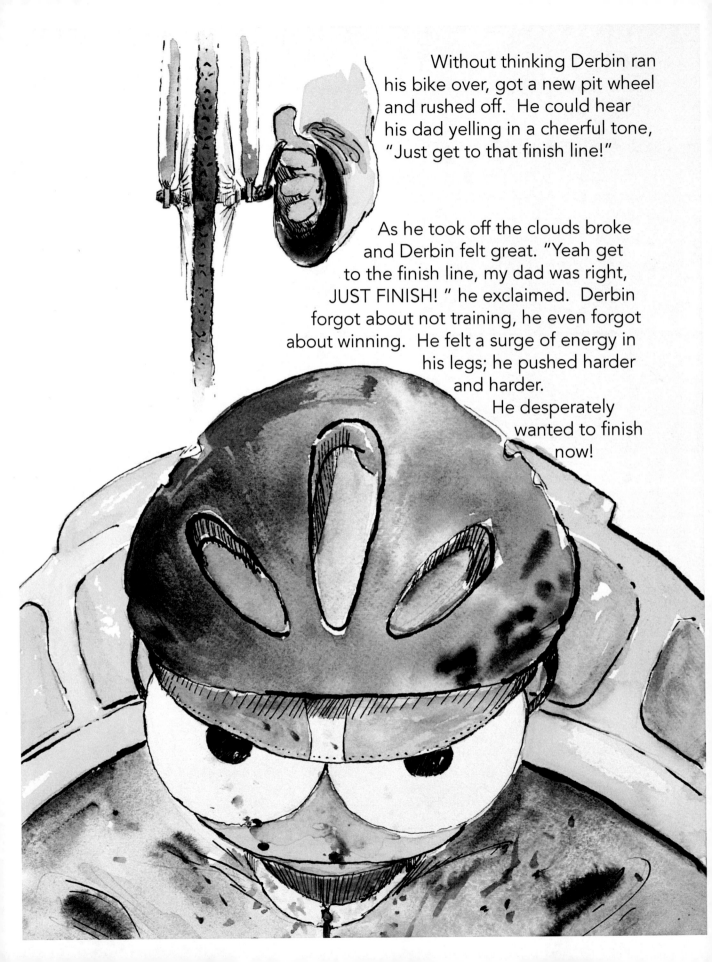

Without thinking Derbin ran his bike over, got a new pit wheel and rushed off. He could hear his dad yelling in a cheerful tone, "Just get to that finish line!"

As he took off the clouds broke and Derbin felt great. "Yeah get to the finish line, my dad was right, JUST FINISH! " he exclaimed. Derbin forgot about not training, he even forgot about winning. He felt a surge of energy in his legs; he pushed harder and harder.
He desperately wanted to finish now!

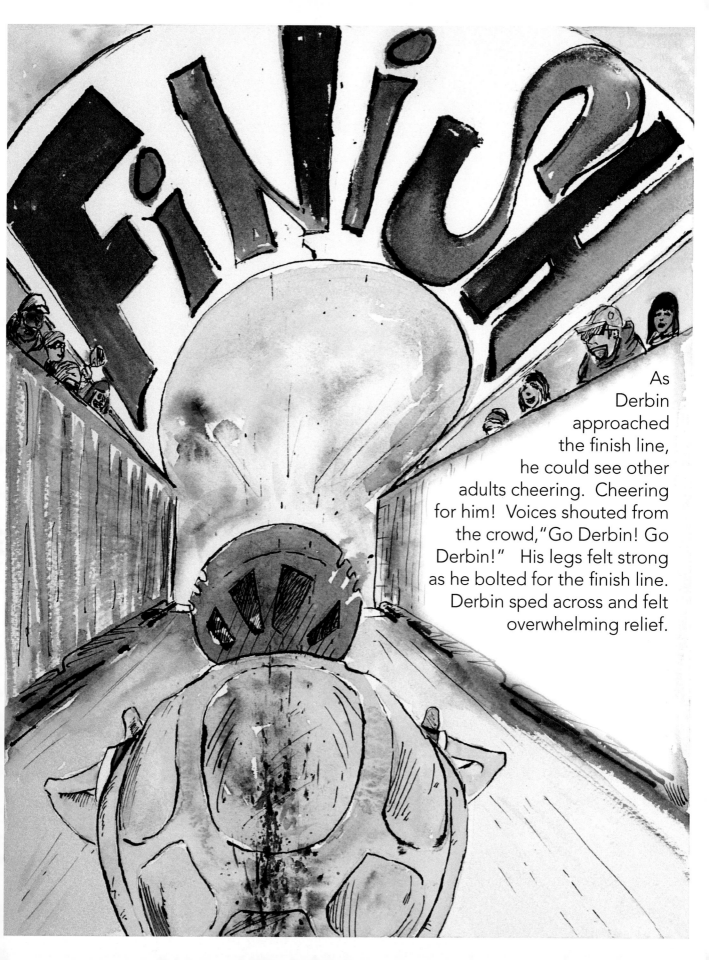

As Derbin approached the finish line, he could see other adults cheering. Cheering for him! Voices shouted from the crowd, "Go Derbin! Go Derbin!" His legs felt strong as he bolted for the finish line. Derbin sped across and felt overwhelming relief.

Derbin found his Dad in the crowd. He jumped into his arms and said, "You were right Dad, I had so much fun!" Then added, "I can't wait for the next race!"

After Derbin cleaned up, he and his Dad found a perfect spot to enjoy lunch and watch the event unfold. Derbin was happy he did his first race and already plans to do another very soon.

The End

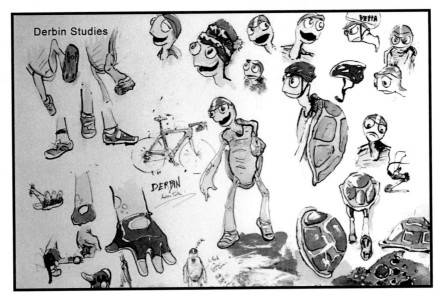

Glossary of Important Cycling Terms

Cyclocross: A fall or winter sport, with specially equipped road style bicycles. The courses are short, with obstacles, and the events have many levels for racers of all ability. They can be very muddy, dry and dusty, or everything in-between. Courses are always lined with tape and usually follow the landscape.

Cyclocross Bicycle: At first glance, most cyclocross bikes look like a regular road style bike. Some people mistakenly call them "10 speeds" but, most have 20-22 gear options. They have special brakes called Cantilevers or even Disk brakes and special tires described below.

Bicycle, essential parts and components.

Barriers: Boards or strips of wood, usually 6 inches in height, that are often placed in pairs. Used in Cyclocross to force the rider to dismount. Some talented riders hop them on the bike!

Cowbell: True to the name, spectators use a cow's bell to ring at the riders and shout encouragement.

Cyclocross Tires: Knobby traction tires for all conditions that allow a rider to slice thru mud or buzz across dry grass. They look very much like mini-mountain bike tires.

Derailleur, Fort and Rear: Both items assist the rider in moving the chain/changing gears.

Flat: That hissing could be a snake, or a "snake bite". Flat tires occur on all bikes, all the time. When a rider has a flat, it's best they know before hand how to fix it. Maybe Derbin could help us with that sometime?

Frame: The supporting structure. Frames come in many sizes to fit many people. Kids bikes come in special sizes too.

Pit Wheel: Usually an extra wheel the racer brings in case of a flat while racing. At times there are wheels for use by all. Extra wheels and bikes are stored in the "**Pit**" area along the course. See pg. 23 for illustration.

Saddle: AKA bike seat. Many sizes and styles.

Run- Up: A steep section that must be ran up, rather then riding up. Very hard.

Cantilever Brakes: A break style that has two "L" brake arms, pulled by a cable in the middle. Each side has a "pad" that rubs the rim.

Start Gun: Some sporting events start with a bang, especially events where there are many people lined up and the start needs to be noisy. The gun shoots blanks.

Stem and Drop Bar: The stem connects the bars to the fork so we can steer. Both have many shapes and sizes available. The bars, usually "ram horn" shaped, allow for various hand positions.